Can the **EVIL SICKLIES** be defeated?

'**GLOOP** is cool, he has a curly bit of hair and likes playing tricks.'

BENJY

Prepare for the **SLIMIEST ADVENTURE** ever!

'I like **BIG BLOB** because he's so slimy and gigantic!'

VEER

OXFORD
UNIVERSITY PRESS

Great Clarendon Street, Oxford OX2 6DP
Oxford University Press is a department of the University of Oxford.
It furthers the University's objective of excellence in research, scholarship,
and education by publishing worldwide. Oxford is a registered trade mark
of Oxford University Press in the UK and in certain other countries

British Library Cataloguing in Publication Data

Data available

ISBN: 978-0-19-276379-2

1 3 5 7 9 10 8 6 4 2

Printed in China

Paper used in the production of this book is a natural,
recyclable product made from wood grown in sustainable forests.
The manufacturing process conforms to the environmental
regulations of the country of origin.

DEXTER GREEN · JAKE DASH

THE GOOZILLAS!

Battle of the Cunge Games

OXFORD
UNIVERSITY PRESS

WELCOME TO THE
WORLD OF
SLIME

SIX **AWESOME** LEVELS TO EXPLORE

Enter a team into the great **GUNGE GAMES**. There are loads of slimy sports to take part in, and win!

Leap from platform to platform, to reach the dizzying heights of the **CRUSTY CRATER**. Whatever you do, don't look down.

It's a dash to the finish line as you speed around this ultimate racing circuit. Can you reach **SLIME CENTRAL** in one piece?

Battle it out in a mission to capture the **FUNGUS FORT**. Beware: you'll need more than ninja skills to defeat the enemies on this level.

Can you escape from the **MONSTROUS MAZE**? Just when you think you're on the right track, the ghostly Gools will be ready to attack.

Dare you enter the dungeon of slime? Watch your step or you just might end up stuck in the **BOG OF BEASTS**!

THE STORY SO FAR

After accidentally **sneezing** all over his tablet computer, Max found himself whisked inside his favourite app, **WORLD OF SLIME**, where he came face-to-face with the Goozillas, a group of green, **slimy** creatures he had created in the game.

When Max discovered that his **sneeze** had destroyed the **GOLDEN GLOB**—a magical artefact that keeps the **WORLD OF SLIME** goo flowing—and that without it the Goozillas' volcano home would completely dry out, he teamed up with his icky new friends and set off to retrieve all the missing pieces, hoping to fix the **GOLDEN GLOB** and bring back the **slime**.

Unfortunately, a group of cutesy-wootsy, sickly-sweet animals from the neighbouring World of Pets app—fed up of having to dress up and play on rainbows all the time—decided they were going to move in to the **slime** volcano.

If the evil Bubble Kitten and her band of Sicklies get the **GOLDEN GLOB** pieces, then it's the end for the Goozillas, and so thanks to that one fateful sneeze, Max has found himself in a frantic race not just to save his new friends, but all of **WORLD OF SLIME** itself!

MEET THE GOOZILLAS

JOE

The joker of the gang. Equipped with special slime-seeking gadget glasses.

GLOOP

The first Goozilla that Max created, and his favourite by far.

ATISHOO

A teeny, baby Goozilla, with an enormous sneeze.

GUNK

A mean, green, fighting machine!

BIG BLOB

Supersized, and super strong, but definitely not super smart.

CAPTAIN CRUST

Old, crusty, and in command.

and the sicklies

BUBBLE KITTEN

The evil leader of the Sicklies. She can blow bubble kisses to trap her enemies.

SUGAR PAWS PUPPY

Bubble Kitten's faithful sidekick. His sticky paw prints will stop you in your tracks.

GLITTER CHICK

Watch out for her eggs-plosive glitterbomb eggs.

DREAMY BUNNY

Beware of her powerful hypnotic gaze.

SQUEAKY GUINEA PIG

His supersonic screech will leave your ears ringing.

SCAMPY HAMSTER

The ultimate kickass, street-fighting, rodent.

CHAPTER
ONE

GARDEN
ATHLETICS

Max stood in the garden, watching reluctantly as his little sister, Amy, hopped and skipped over several obstacles she'd set out across the grass.

With a **WHOOP**, Amy made the final jump, then thrust her arms in the air and shouted, 'Stop the clock!'

Sighing, Max tapped the screen of his tablet computer, pausing the stopwatch function.

'Eleven seconds,' he said.

'New world record!' Amy cheered. She bounced up and down. 'OK, now for the flying disc throwing event!'

'You mean the discus,' Max corrected, as Amy grabbed a circle of plastic from the grass. 'And anyway, that's not a discus, it's a frisbee.'

WHEEE!

The frisbee whistled towards Max, then thonked him on the head.

'Ow! Watch it!' he cried.

'Whoops! Sorry . . . I'll be more careful,' Amy replied, snatching the fallen frisbee. She tossed it again. It *ROCKETED* upwards and got stuck in the branches of their neighbour's tree.

'You call that careful?' Max sighed.

'Go and get it, Max!' Amy said.

Max leaned back and looked up at

the frisbee. It was way up near the top of the tree, snagged on one of the thinner branches. Max swallowed, and felt his stomach knot up in panic.

'It's too high. I'll never reach it,' he said.

'What's the matter? Are you scared?' Amy teased.

Max scowled. 'No!' he lied. 'I'm just . . . bored, that's all. I want to go inside.'

That wasn't quite true, either. Max was bored, but that wasn't why he wanted to go inside. Ever since **sneezing** himself into the **WORLD OF SLIME** video game and meeting the Goozillas, he'd dedicated himself to helping them. That first **sneeze** had broken the magical **GOLDEN GLOB**, the power source that kept the **WORLD OF SLIME** volcano nice and **gooey**, and Max had now helped the Goozillas find five of the six missing pieces.

He desperately wanted to get back there

4

and find that sixth piece, but he was stuck here instead, watching Amy playing her silly Garden Athletics.

'Oh no, how did that happen?' asked Mum, appearing from inside the house and staring up at the frisbee.

'I'll give you three guesses,' said Max, glancing at Amy.

'Max is too scared to climb up and get it,' Amy retorted.

'I am not!' Max protested. 'I could climb up there if I wanted to. Yesterday, I even . . .'

He stopped himself. He couldn't exactly reveal to Mum and Amy that yesterday he'd been hopping from platform to platform in the **WORLD OF SLIME**.

5

Or that he'd made the mistake of looking down from near the top, and discovered that he was really quite scared of heights.

'Why don't we play a different game?' Mum suggested. 'Like racing, or hurdles?'

Max groaned. 'Do we have to?' He looked longingly down at the tablet in his hands.

'Fine,' she said, and then smiled. 'Off you go and play your game. If you change your mind, you know where to find us.'

Amy began to jump up and down. 'Ooh! Ooh! I know what we can do next. Pole vault!'

6

Max saw a look of concern flash over his mum's face, before he slipped into the house and hurried up the stairs. He still felt a bit embarrassed about being too scared to climb the tree, but he knew he'd feel better once he was inside the **WORLD OF SLIME**.

Racing into his room, he closed the door, jumped onto his bed, and removed the little pepper sachet he'd stashed under his pillow the night before.

A quick tap on the tablet shut down the stopwatch timer and brought him back to the main screen. The **WORLD OF SLIME** icon sat right in the centre. Another prod opened it up, and it had barely finished loading when Max held the open pepper packet under one nostril and sniffed.

His eyes **WATERED**.

His nose **ITCHED**.

He felt the tingling that told him he was going to—

ATCHOO!

A spray of snot hit the screen and began to sizzle and pop. The ceiling twirled around until it became the floor, and Max's bed looped and plunged as if it were on a roller coaster track.

The walls turned gungy. The curtains

became long strings of snot. Max half-cheered, half-screamed as he plunged through his bed and landed with a plop in the **WORLD OF** . . .

Wait a minute.

Max blinked. He'd expected to find himself inside the Goozillas' volcano, but instead he was sitting on a patch of grass beneath a bright blue sky.

'OK,' he mumbled, blinking in the dazzling sunshine. 'Where am I?'

CHAPTER TWO

SPEARED

A shadow passed over Max as the sun went
behind a mountain.

No, not a mountain, Max realized.
From down on the grass it just looked
like a mountain. It was **squidgier** than a
mountain, though. Greener, too. The sun
shone through its slimy frame, making it
glow.

'Big Blob!' said Max, leaping to his feet.

'Where?' said Big Blob, frowning. Blob
was the largest and strongest of all the
Goozillas, but definitely not the smartest.
'Oh. Wait. That's me,' he said. He waved.

'Hello Max.'

If Big Blob was here, then maybe this was the **WORLD OF SLIME**, after all. Max was just about to ask when something long and sharp squelched through Big Blob's back and stuck out through his front. The pointed tip stopped just centimetres from Max's nose. His eyes crossed as he tried to get a proper look at it.

At first, he thought it was a spear, but when he looked closer he realized it was a javelin. Big Blob had a javelin sticking all the way through him! Max thought it must hurt, but Blob didn't even seem to have noticed.

'Whoops! Sorry!' called a voice from somewhere behind the giant Goozilla.

Gloop, the first Goozilla Max had ever created, slid over. His green face blushed red as he heaved the javelin out. It made a loud

FAAAART

noise as it pulled free of Big Blob's squidgy body.

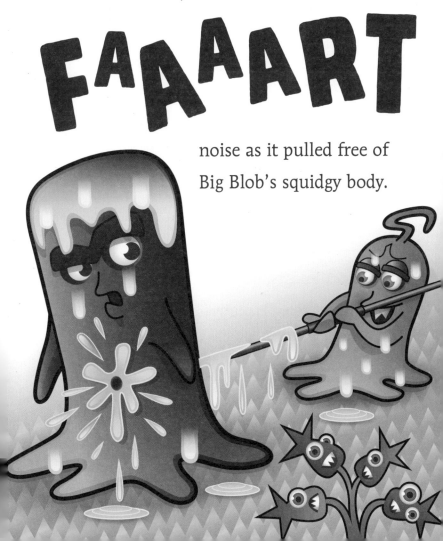

'Pardon me,' said Blob, looking confused. Mind you, he always looked confused, so there was nothing new there.

'Gloop!' said Max, smiling at his little friend. 'What's going on? Where are we?'

'CRUSTY CRATER,' replied Gloop. He didn't look particularly happy, and Max quickly worked out why.

'The **Battle of the Gunge Games**,' groaned Max. 'This is the game's final stage. Of course.'

'Woo. Sports,' Gloop muttered. He rolled his eyes. 'Hooray.'

When Max had made Gloop, he'd based the Goozilla on himself. He was good at the same things as Max, and terrible at the same things, too. Top of the list of things they were terrible at was sports.

It wasn't that they didn't enjoy watching sports—Max liked a bit of footy on the TV as much as anyone—they just weren't very good at the taking part bit. Max hoped getting the final **GOLDEN GLOB** piece wouldn't rely on his sporting talents, otherwise they were in trouble.

Big Blob shuffled aside to reveal the rest of **CRUSTY CRATER**. It was a huge bowl-shaped area right at the top of the volcano, with a hole in the centre where the **slime** was supposed to shoot up. Before the **GOLDEN GLOB** had been destroyed, the **slime** would splurt up through the crater like a fountain, drizzling goo over the running track and grass of the **Gunge Games** level.

Now, though, the running track was dry and crusty, and even the artificial grass looked in danger of withering away.

As Max looked around the dried-out crater, he spotted the rest of the Goozillas. They were all hard at work practising various sporting activities. Joe was doing star jumps, which made his Gadget Glasses bounce up and down on his face.

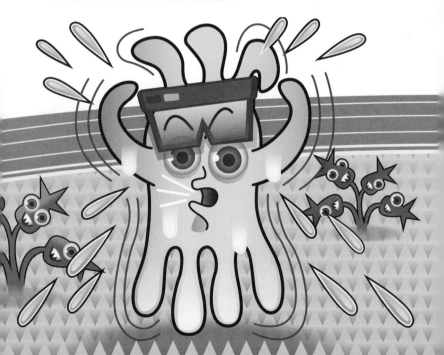

They weren't exactly like star jumps, because the Goozillas didn't have long enough legs, so Joe was really just jumping up and down and waving his arms around.

Captain Crust, the oldest of the Goozillas, was supporting himself on his SnotShooter cane as he stretched and did squats. Beside him, Gunk had put down his **slime** gun and was rattling through some push-ups.

'Two-hundred-and-six . . .' he counted. 'Two-hundred-and-seven . . .'

'More like twenty-seven, if he's lucky,' Gloop whispered, and Max giggled.

A little further away, the smallest Goozilla, Atishoo, hopped over a row of hurdles, making little '**HUP!**' sounds with every jump.

Max smiled. It was good to see his friends again. The feeling was quickly replaced by anger, though, when he spotted the other team training on the far side of the crater.

'Bubble Kitten and the **Sicklies**!' he spat. 'What are they doing here?'

'Do you really have to ask?' said Gloop. He pointed over to a trophy cabinet. There, locked inside, was the final piece of the **GOLDEN GLOB**.

'The **GLOB** piece!' Max gasped.

'Take a good long look,' purred Bubble Kitten, appearing silently behind the Goozillas. **'THIS IS AS CLOSE AS YOU'RE GOING TO GET.'**

19

The wicked feline gestured back towards the **Sicklies**, who were all training hard. 'We're going to win your pointless little games, and then the **GLOB** piece will be ours.'

'Ha! No way,' Max said, clenching his fists. 'We've already beaten you to five of them.'

'Oh, I know,' said Bubble Kitten. 'But we only need one piece to stop you fixing the **GOLDEN GLOB**, and then your precious **WORLD OF SLIME** will dry out, and we'll move right in.'

Her eyes narrowed and her mouth drew up in a hiss.

'THIS PLACE WILL BE OURS, GOO-LOSERS.

JUST YOU WAIT.'

Laughing, Bubble Kitten whirled around, and trotted back to join her minions. Max felt his heart sink as he watched her go. He was rubbish at sports. Gloop was rubbish at sports. He wasn't sure about the others, but considering Captain Crust couldn't bend down without making a crunching noise, he didn't fancy their chances.

It wasn't fair. They'd come all this way, collected all those **GLOB** pieces, and now they would almost certainly fall at the final hurdle.

Literally.

CHAPTER THREE

RUNNING BLIND

While Bubble Kitten rejoined her gang, the other Goozillas spotted Max and hurried over to welcome him. They were all puffing and panting, and Max could barely understand them as they wheezed out their hellos.

'Thank . . . goo-ness . . . you're . . . here,' Captain Crust croaked. 'Now perhaps . . . we stand . . . a chance.'

He sat down on a box of sports equipment, trying to get his breath back.

'Yeah, we're all pretty hopeless,' said Joe, his **slime** shiny with sweat, 'but we're bound to win now that you're here.'

'Uh . . . about that,' stuttered Max, shooting Gloop a sideways glance.

But before he could say any more, a whirring sound came from above. A silver sphere with a big camera-like lens on one side and a screen on the other flew down towards them. Captain Crust sighed with relief as the sphere's spinning rotor blade blew cool air over him and the others.

The **Battle of the Gunge Games** level wasn't Max's favourite, but he knew a R E F B o T when he saw one. The little flying devices were responsible for making sure everyone played fairly and didn't cheat. With Bubble Kitten and the **Sicklies** taking part, it was going to have its work cut out for it.

'WELCOME, COMPETITORS!' the REFBOT said, its voice chiming from a speaker somewhere inside it. 'AND WELCOME, SPECTATORS.'

Max frowned. 'Spectators?'

He turned just as a circle of stadium seating rose from the ground all around the edges of the volcano's crater. There were hundreds of seats, and in each one sat a different Goozilla.

Well, technically they weren't all that different. Max recognized them as all the unfinished characters he'd started creating, but then got a bit bored of.

There were Goozillas with one eye, Goozillas with no arms, and Goozillas with . . . well, nothing at all. Those ones just looked like giant bogies.

He hadn't spent many personality points on any of them, so they just sat silently in their seats, doing very little. A couple of them cheered, but it was half-hearted, as if they weren't quite sure what they were cheering for. Or, for that matter, where they even were.

Right there and then, Max vowed to finish every single Goozilla in the audience. First, though, they had to get that **GLOB** piece.

'Welcome to the **Gunge Games**!' the REFBOT announced. 'The ultimate test of speed, strength, skill, stamina, and—'

'Yes, yes, get on with it,' cried Bubble Kitten. She sneered over at Max and the others. 'Some of us have a **GLOB** piece to win.'

Bubble Kitten's sidekick, Sugar Paws Puppy, leaned in closer. 'Who's that, then?'

'Us, you dolt!'

'Oh. Right. Yeah.'

'VERY WELL,' said the REFBOT. 'OUR FIRST EVENT IS . . .'

Lots of symbols flashed up on its screen, too quickly to make out properly. Then there was a ding as one symbol began to flash.

'HURDLES!'

'AND OUR FIRST COMPETITORS ARE . . .'

This time, the faces of Max and the Goozillas all

29

flashed across the screen, there one second, gone the next. Max crossed his fingers.

'Please not me, please not me, please not me,' he whispered. Beside him, Gloop did exactly the same.

'Yes!' Gloop cried, as Joe's face flashed up on the REFBOT's display. 'It isn't me!'

'Don't speak too soon,' said Max, pointing to the track. 'There are six lanes, so that means three from each team.'

Gloop gulped. 'Oh . . . great.'

He and Max both shuffled anxiously as more faces appeared on the REFBOT's screen. Gunk was the next Goozilla chosen to take part.

'Ha!' he snorted, limbering up. 'We've got this in the bag.'

30

Another face flashed up. Everyone stared at the image of Captain Crust.

'No, wait. We're doomed,' Gunk muttered.

'Nonsense!' said the captain. 'Since absorbing that last **GLOB** piece, I feel twenty years younger.'

'That still makes you a hundred and seven,' Gunk pointed out.

'Oh,' said the old Goozilla, his smile fading. 'Yes. Good point.'

A cheer rose up from the **Sicklies** as Dreamy Bunny's face appeared on screen. The fluffy white rabbit bounded over to the starting line in two huge hops.

Gunk groaned. 'Yep. Totally doomed.'

Two more **Sicklies** were chosen—

Squeaky Guinea Pig and Scampy Hamster—
then the REFBOT let out a shrill whistle
sound.

'COMPETITORS, TAKE YOUR
POSITIONS!' it instructed.

'Wait!' said Bubble Kitten, holding up a
clawed hand. She pointed to the Goozillas.
'They have an advantage.'

'An advantage?' Gunk snorted. 'We're in
a jumping race against a giant bunny. How
is that an advantage?'

'His Gadget Glasses,' said Bubble Kitten,
scowling at Joe. 'They do . . . things. They're
a mechanical aid, so they
aren't allowed.'

'How? I don't jump
with my eyes,' said Joe.

'BUBBLE KITTEN IS CORRECT,' said the REFBOT. 'THOSE GLASSES COULD ALLOW YOU TO PLOT THE FASTEST AND MOST EFFICIENT ROUTE OVER THE OBSTACLES. THEREFORE, YOU MUST REMOVE THEM.'

Joe blinked. 'But how will I see?'

Bubble Kitten sniggered. 'Not our problem.'

Reluctantly, Joe removed his Gadget Glasses and handed them to Gloop. At least, he thought he handed them to Gloop, but as Gloop was now just a blurry green shape to him, he couldn't be sure.

He and the other Goozillas took their positions. Gunk had to turn Joe so he was facing the right way. Sugar Paws and

Scampy crouched on the starting blocks like sprinters. Dreamy Bunny, on the other hand, stood upright, impatiently tapping a large fluffy foot.

'ON YOUR MARKS. GET SET,' began the REFBOT. Joe squinted and peered along the track. He could just make out the hurdles ahead of him.

'GO!'

The two unfinished Goozillas who had cheered earlier, cheered again. Dreamy Bunny kicked off from the starting line with a **BOING**, clearing two hurdles in one go.

Joe lurched forwards just as the other Goozillas began to run. Unable to see properly, he immediately veered off to the left, and thudded sideways into Gunk.

'Hey, watch it!' Gunk protested. Off-balance, he crashed into Captain Crust, and all three Goozillas spun and tumbled into a big quivering heap of goo on the track.

Scampy and Squeaky pulled ahead, but that didn't matter. At the other end of the track, Dreamy Bunny had already bounded across the finish line, winning the race.

'Like I said,' Gunk muttered from inside the pile of Goozillas. 'Doomed.'

CHAPTER FOUR

TUG-OF-WHOA!

'ROUND ONE GOES TO THE SICKLIES,' the REFBOT announced, and Bubble Kitten's crew all laughed and cheered and pulled faces at the Goozillas.

'Sorry, guys,' said Joe, putting his glasses back on. 'I let you down.'

'No, you didn't,' said Max.

'Uh, yes he did,' said Gunk.

The others all glared at him. 'Uh, I mean . . . no, you didn't,' Gunk grunted. He tried to smile, but he wasn't very good at it.

'Thanks, everyone,' said Joe. 'Hopefully we'll win the next one.'

As if on cue, the REFBOT's screen lit up. 'AND OUR SECOND EVENT,' it announced, as the symbols flashed by again, 'IS THE TUG-OF-WAR!'

The Goozillas' faces all flickered on screen again. The real Goozillas all watched, waiting to see who would be chosen.

'It's going to be me, isn't it?' said Atishoo, glumly. He wasn't just the smallest Goozilla, he also had no arms, which would make the Tug-of-War rather tricky. 'I bet it's going to be me.'

Max and his friends all held their breath as their faces appeared in quick succession. While Max wasn't exactly keen to do the Tug-of-War, he'd have a better chance than

Atishoo, at least. Still, if they
were very lucky, it would be—

'Big Blob!' cried Gloop.

'What?' said Big Blob.

'It's you!' laughed Max.
'You've been chosen!'

'I have?' said the giant Goozilla. 'Oh.'

Several seconds passed.

'What for?'

'For the Tug-of-War, old chap,' said
Captain Crust. 'And those **Sicklies** don't
look very happy about it!'

That was an understatement. The
Sicklies had all gone pale and now stood
staring at Big Blob with their mouths
hanging open.

'Not so confident now, are you?' Gloop laughed.

'IN THE INTERESTS OF FAIRNESS, THIS WILL BE A BALANCED EVENT,' the REFBOT announced.

Max frowned. 'What does that mean?'

The answer came soon enough. Instead of just one Sicklie's face appearing on the REFBOT's screen, they all appeared at once.

'Hold on. One versus six? That seems a tad unfair!' Captain Crust protested.

'NEGATIVE,' the REFBOT replied. 'BOTH TEAMS ARE NOW EVENLY MATCHED FOR WEIGHT. COMPETITORS, TAKE YOUR POSITIONS.'

A long rope had been placed on the ground, stretching across a pool of bubbling **slime**. Whoever lost the Tug-of-War would be pulled into the **slime**, and Bubble Kitten stared nervously down into it as she took up her position. The other

Sicklies gathered behind her, each holding tightly to the rope.

'OK, Blob, pick up the rope,' Joe instructed.

Blob looked puzzled. 'All of it?'

'No, just grab that bit next to you and hold onto it as tight as you can,' said Joe, pointing.

Blob bent slowly and gripped the rope. As soon as he had, the REFBOT blasted its whistle. The rope between the Sicklies and Big Blob was pulled tight, as the villainous pets began to puff and pant with effort.

Around the crater, the audience watched in near-silence. Even they seemed surprised, though, when Big Blob was pulled half a step closer to the pit.

'What?!' Gunk spluttered. 'How is that possible?'

'How can they be beating Blob?' Gloop gasped.

'Maybe there are too many of them, even for him,' Atishoo squeaked.

Max wasn't so sure, though. He took a step closer to the giant Goozilla.

'Uh, Blob,' he said.

Big Blob blinked, as if waking from a dream. 'Yeah?'

'You do know you're supposed to be pulling, yes?'

Blob looked down at the rope in his hands, then over at the **Sicklies**, who were turning red with effort. Finally, Blob

looked back at Max again.

'Am I?'

'Indeed you are,' confirmed Captain Crust.

'What, this thing?'

Max nodded. 'The rope. Yes.'

'Oh.'

Blob thought for

a moment, then he gave a short, sharp tug on the rope. The **Sicklies** screamed as they were jerked off their feet and straight into the pit.

Max jumped back as a series of gloopy sploshes sprayed goo in all directions.

Big Blob looked over at Max and Captain Crust. 'Like that?' he asked.

The captain watched Bubble Kitten and the other **Sicklies** thrashing and squealing in the **slime** pit. 'Yes, Blob,' he said, grinning beneath his moustache. 'Exactly like that!'

CHAPTER FIVE

NEW ARRIVAL

Max and the others spent a few seconds congratulating Big Blob. The giant Goozilla looked like he didn't quite understand what all the fuss was about, but he seemed to be enjoying the attention, all the same.

'One all!' Gunk announced.

'AND NOW, IT'S TIME FOR THE NEXT EVENT,' said the REFBOT. A symbol flashed up on its screen. 'THE THREE-LEGGED RACE!'

A high-pitched alarm sounded. At first, Max panicked, thinking it was the screen time alert on his tablet, but then a series of colourful lights flickered across the REFBOT. 'THIS IS AN ALL PLAY EVENT!' it announced. 'ALL MEMBERS OF EACH TEAM WILL TAKE PART!'

'Wait,' said Gloop. 'We're all racing?'

'Looks like it,' said Max.

'Against us,' said Bubble Kitten, gesturing to herself and the Sicklies. 'You may as well give up now. I mean, how can you win a three-legged race when most of you barely even have legs?'

'She's right,' Gloop whispered, watching the REFBOT tie a rope around one of Sugar Paws Puppy's legs, then loop it around one of Bubble Kitten's. 'I'm hopeless at this sort of thing.'

'We'll be fine,' said Max. 'We can do this.'

There was a muttering from behind them, and Max realized the other Goozillas were having doubts, too. 'She's right,' Joe said. 'We don't have proper legs.'

'We've got something better,' said Max.

'Arms?' Gunk guessed.

'Speak for yourself,' said Atishoo.

'Each other,' Max said. 'You know how we've got all the **GLOB** pieces so far? By working together. This is no different.'

He looked down as the REFBOT tied a rope around one of his ankles, then looped it around Gloop's much shorter leg.

'We can do this. I know we can,' Max said. 'We just have to believe in ourselves. If we do that, we can do anything.'

The others nodded, slowly at first, but

becoming more confident. 'Dash it, you're right,' said Captain Crust. He squidged up next to Gunk. 'Let's all partner up and win this thing!'

'Can't I go with Joe?' Gunk asked, but the captain just slapped him on the back and laughed.

'That's the spirit, old boy!'

The REFBOT tied their legs together, then did the same to Big Blob and Joe. Atishoo perched on Joe's head. The two of them combined still weren't as tall as Blob.

Max and the Goozillas half-walked, half-hopped to the starting line. The race was just fifty metres from start to finish. No distance at all, really. Max clenched his fists and gritted his teeth. They could do this. They could win!

Bubble Kitten and Sugar Paws trotted up to the starting line. They were each walking on four legs, so having one tied together wasn't slowing them down much. The other Sicklies joined them, and soon both teams were lined up and ready.

Max met Gloop's nervous gaze. 'Win or

lose, we'll do it together,' he said, and the two friends shook hands.

'Together,' Gloop agreed.

'ON YOUR MARKS,' began the REFBOT. Max put an arm around Gloop's shoulder, and Gloop did the same to him.

'GET SET!'

'Good luck, chaps!' hollered Captain Crust.

'See you at the finish line, slimeballs,' Bubble Kitten snorted.

'GO!'

A whistle blew, and the race got underway. Max and Gloop *RAN* like they'd never *RUN* before—tied together with a bit of rope, and sort of skipping and jumping with every second step.

Most of the **Sicklies** quickly pulled ahead, making a **DASH** towards the finish line. Only Bubble Kitten and Sugar Paws seemed to be struggling. They were falling behind the rest of the pack, and weren't far ahead of Max and Gloop.

'Careful, old chap!' Captain Crust protested, as Gunk tried to speed up. 'You'll pull my leg off!'

Max glanced back over his shoulder to see Gunk and the captain trip over and collapse on top of one another.

'**NOT AGAIN!**' Gunk yelped.

Meanwhile, Big Blob had failed to hear the starting whistle, and was still at the starting line. Joe was shouting and doing his best to drag Blob along, but the biggest Goozilla hadn't moved a millimetre.

'It's all up to us!' Max said.

'It's no good, Max,' Gloop said. 'I'm useless at sports.'

'We both are,' said Max. 'But we just need the right motivation. Think about the **GLOB** piece. Think about what will happen if Bubble Kitten wins.'

Gloop's eyes went wide. His jaw dropped.

'You're right. We can't let her get it! Let's move!'

Max yelped in surprise as Gloop sped up. The Goozilla began bounding along the track, dragging Max with him, and it was all Max could do to hop along beside him.

'We're gaining on them! We're gaining!' said Max. Bubble Kitten and Sugar Paws were just ahead now, weaving from side to side across the track. The other Sicklies and the finish line were a little further beyond them. Max felt a surge of hope. They were going to make it. They were going to—

BOoOOOlNG.

Max and Gloop both came to a sudden stop. The ground beneath them was sticky, making it impossible for either of them to move.

'What's going on?' Gloop asked. 'We're stuck!'

Max looked down and spotted several big sticky paw-prints on the track beneath them. 'Sugar Paws!' he groaned.

Sure enough, Bubble Kitten and her sidekick were both looking back, grinning broadly. 'Oh dear, what a shame,' the wicked kitty sniggered. She raised a paw and gave them a wave. '**TOODLE-OO**.'

Then she and Sugar Paws broke into a sprint, crossing the finish line right behind the rest of the Sicklies.

'ROUND
THREE
TO THE
SICKLIES!'

the REFBOT announced,
and Max heard Gloop let out a groan. They
had lost another round. They were falling
behind, and the **GLOB** piece was further
away than ever.

CHAPTER SIX

FRIEND TO FOE

Once everyone was untied, Max and the Goozillas plodded back to the starting line. Except Joe, Atishoo, and Big Blob, who had never even left it.

'So much for believing in ourselves,' said Gunk.

'It's not fair, we could have won,' Max insisted. 'If those cheats hadn't used Sugar Paws's sticky paw prints to slow us down.'

'And now they've faded away,' said Gloop. 'So we can't even prove it to the ref.'

'Oh, hard lines, you guys,' said Bubble

Kitten, appearing beside them. She grinned, showing off her sharp teeth. 'Looks like you won't be getting that **GLOB** piece after all.'

'There are still two rounds left,' Max reminded her.

'And we intend to win them both,' the cat hissed. 'Then this place will be ours for the taking.'

She skipped away, sniggering. Gunk growled and reached for his SplutShooter gun, but an announcement from the REFBOT stopped him covering Bubble Kitten in green **gunge**.

'OUR NEXT EVENT IS A ONE ON ONE EVENT,' the REFBOT said. An icon flashed up on its screen. 'WRESTLING!'

Gunk clenched his fists. 'Oh, please let it be me. Let me have a shot at one of those guys.'

The faces of Max and the Goozillas flicked by. After what felt like a long time, it stopped on one.

'Oh,' said Gloop.

'Ooh boy,' said Max.

Gunk groaned. 'You have got to be kidding me.'

'Wait, that's me!' said Atishoo, just before his face was replaced with that of the karate-kicking Scampy Hamster.

'**YES!**' roared Bubble Kitten. '**IN YOUR FACES, GOO-LOSERS!**'

The ground rumbled beneath everyone's feet. Max jumped in fright. Was the volcano about to erupt? Had the **slime** somehow returned?

But no. Instead of a fountain of green goo, a wrestling ring rose up out of a hatch in the grass. The REFBOT hovered above it and instructed Scampy and Atishoo to take their places.

Atishoo bounced into the ring between the top and middle ropes. On the other side of the ring, Scampy somersaulted over the top rope and landed in a ninja pose.

Max gulped. 'Are you sure you want to do this?' he asked.

Atishoo smiled back at him. 'Hey, I might be small, but I pack a punch!'

'Except you don't have fists,' Gunk pointed out. 'Or arms.'

'Trust me,' said Atishoo. 'I'll be fine.'

The bell announcing the start of the match rang. Scampy pounced, launching himself into an impressive flying kick.

Atishoo winked at Max.

'Be right back,' he said, then he sneezed. The force of the sneeze shot him backwards, and he hit

Scampy right in the middle of his face.

The hamster toppled over and slammed onto the canvas, his hands covering his face. 'Ow! My nose! He hit me on my nose! Is that allowed?'

'Of course it's allowed, you dolt!' Bubble Kitten spat. **'NOW GET UP!'**

Scampy got to his feet just as Atishoo bounced off the top rope and went streaking back the way he'd come. He thudded into the back of Scampy's head, knocking the hamster off his feet again.

'Aargh! I don't like this! I want out!' Scampy sobbed.

Atishoo bounced from rope to rope, criss-crossing through the air above the fallen hamster's head. Scampy's eyes rolled as he

tried to follow Atishoo's dizzying flight. The
REFBOT closed in, watching carefully. The
little Goozilla just had to pin Scampy, and
another round was in the bag.

'Great work, Atishoo!' Max cried.

'Didn't doubt you for a minute,' cheered
Gunk.

Suddenly, an **EXPLOSION** echoed
around the crater from somewhere behind
them. The Goozillas and the
REFBOT all turned to see
Glitter Chick standing a short
distance away in a cloud of
glitter.

'Whoops! Sorry,' she said in
her gruff, booming voice. 'One of
my eggs exploded.'

While the Goozillas were distracted, Bubble Kitten jumped into the ring with a folding metal chair. She held it up in front of Atishoo as he flew across the ring. This would stop him in his tracks! There was a loud **CLANG** as he hit the metal.

But instead of halting the flying Goozilla, the force of his impact made the chair swing back and thwack Bubble Kitten in the face with a **CLANG!**

She staggered backwards, hit the top rope of the ring, then fell over the top.

Atishoo dropped onto the canvas, then hopped onto Scampy Hamster's chest just as the REFBOT turned its camera eye back towards the ring. Scampy whimpered, but was still too dizzy to break free as numbers flashed on the REFBOT's screen.

'ONE,' it chimed. 'TWO. THREE!'

The Goozillas cheered in triumph. Atishoo bounced off Scampy's chest, flipped in the air, then sneezed his way back over to join his friends.

Four events in, and the games
were now neck and neck. As Atishoo and
the Goozillas celebrated, Max looked over
to the trophy cabinet with the **GOLDEN
GLOB** piece inside. There was just one event
to go. One event that would decide the fate
of the **WORLD OF SLIME**.

Max nodded and clenched his fists.
'Bring it on!'

CHAPTER SEVEN

THE PIT OF SLIME

A hush fell over the crater as icons flashed on the REFBOT's screen. Max held his breath. He almost couldn't bring himself to look as he waited to see what event would be next.

'AND OUR FINAL EVENT,' said the REFBOT, in a voice that was barely a whisper. 'IS ANOTHER ONE ON ONE COMPETITION . . .'

From somewhere inside the REFBOT there came a drumroll sound. Gloop swallowed. 'Come on, be something good. Be something good.'

The screen stopped flickering and settled on a single icon. It showed a rectangle above a larger rectangle. Max had no idea what it was supposed to be.

'SLIME DIVING!' the REFBOT announced.

'Yes!' cheered Joe. 'Goozillas are awesome at Slime Diving!'

'YUCK!' spat Bubble Kitten. 'One of us? Dive into **slime**? Disgusting.'

'You can always give up,' Max suggested.

Bubble Kitten scowled. 'Oh, I think not.'

'ONE COMPETITOR WILL BE CHOSEN FROM EACH TEAM,' the REFBOT explained. 'THEY WILL EACH JUMP FROM THE DIVING BOARD AND INTO THE POOL OF SLIME. POINTS

74

WILL BE AWARDED FOR STYLE, TECHNICAL ABILITY, AND THE BIGGEST SPLOOSH. COMPETING FOR THE SICKLIES WILL BE . . .'

Faces flashed on the REFBOT's screen again, then quickly stopped. 'BUBBLE KITTEN!'

'Ugh!' Bubble Kitten hissed, but then she shook her head. 'Fine. You want to see diving, I'll show you diving! Besides, I suppose it's appropriate that I'm the one to finally defeat you all.'

The Goozillas' competitor was chosen

next. They stood together, watching the faces appear. The Goozillas seemed relaxed and confident. Even Gloop was smiling. They were all great at Slime Diving.

Max's eyes widened in surprise when he saw his own face smiling down from the screen.

'Wait, what?' he said. 'It's me? *I* have to do a high-dive?'

He thought back to that scary moment up on the platforms, looking at the ground far below, and shuddered. He hoped the diving board wasn't too high off the—

'WHOA!' cried Gunk, as the board rose up out of the ground behind them. It stretched up, up, up, getting higher and higher until it was almost lost among the clouds.

When it had finally locked into position, part of the ground slid aside, revealing a small pool filled with gloopy green **gunge**. It was roughly three bathtubs long by five wide, and Max had a horrible vision of himself missing it completely and going splat on the ground.

'Oooo-kay,' he whispered, leaning back and looking up at the diving board. 'That is high.'

'BUBBLE KITTEN TO JUMP FIRST,' said the REFBOT.

'Watch and learn, Goo-losers,' she said, as she jumped onto the ladder and began to climb.

Bubble Kitten moved quickly, but it still took her almost a full two minutes to reach the top.

'If we're lucky, she'll fall off,' Gunk said. They all watched as the evil kitty bounced once on the diving board, sprung upwards, performed a spinning pirouette in the air, then flipped twice and unfurled

herself into a perfect diving position.

The **Sicklies** cheered and applauded as they watched their leader plunge gracefully downwards. Even Max had to admit it was an impressive sight, although the elegant effect was slightly ruined by the loud **FAAAART** sound she made as she landed in the pool of **gunge**.

For a moment, nothing happened, but then Bubble Kitten leaped out of the goo and up onto solid ground. She looked smaller than normal with her fur all matted down by the **slime**.

'Beat that!' she said, spitting out a mouthful of **gunge**. She waddled over to join her team. 'Now, if you'll excuse me, I need a bath.'

Max couldn't help but giggle as Bubble Kitten sat down and began licking herself clean. From the expression on her face, the **slime** tasted as bad as it looked.

80

He soon stopped laughing, though, when he saw the score Bubble Kitten had been awarded.

'Twenty points,' he groaned. 'How am I supposed to beat that?'

'You can do it, Max,' said Gloop.

'Yeah,' agreed Joe. 'We believe in you.'

'Even me,' said Gunk. 'And I am not a trusting person.'

Max took a deep breath. He looked around at his friends, then at all the other Goozillas watching from the stands. They were counting on him. The whole **WORLD OF SLIME** was counting on him.

'I can do this,' he whispered.

And then, he began to climb.

CHAPTER EIGHT

THE DIVE

It took Max a long time to reach the top of the ladder. When he finally pulled himself up onto the diving board, he was too scared to stand up. The wind whistled around him, nudging him left and right as he crawled along the board.

At last, he reached the end of the diving board and risked a peek over the edge. Big mistake! The ground was a loooooong way away. The pool looked smaller than a postage stamp from way up there, and the Goozillas were bogey-sized green blobs around it.

'I c-can't do it,' Max whispered, gripping the board until his knuckles turned white. 'It's no use.'

He hugged the board, too terrified to move. Jumping from platform to platform the day before had been one thing, but jumping from this height was crazy.

He was about to shout down to the Goozillas that he was too scared to jump when he heard a sound drifting up from below. Cheering. Lots of cheering.

'MA-AX! MA-AX! MA-AX!'

At first, Max thought it was just his friends, but as it grew louder he realized it couldn't possibly just be them. Swallowing nervously, he raised his head a little and saw that all the unfinished Goozillas were

84

standing up. Those that had eyes were looking up at him, and those that had mouths were chanting his name.

'Hey, Max,' came a voice from behind him.

Max screamed in fright and almost fell off. When he was sure he had a grip on the board, he looked back to see Atishoo at the top of the ladder.

The little Goozilla nodded down at

the spectators far below. 'It's like you said—you just have to believe in yourself. Everyone down there believes in you.' He frowned. 'Well, maybe not the Sicklies, but everyone who counts. We all know you can do it.'

Max shook his head. 'But it's so high! If I hit the ground, I won't bounce. I'm not like you. I'm not a Goozilla.'

'Are you kidding me?' Atishoo said. 'You're the greatest Goozilla of all. If anyone can do this, it's you.'

Max felt a flutter in his belly, like lots of butterflies waking up. Over the sound of the cheering, he heard another sound— the sound of Bubble Kitten laughing. She was going to get the **GLOB** piece. She was going to rule the **WORLD OF SLIME**. She was going to banish his friends from their home forever.

'No!' said Max out loud, gritting his teeth. 'She isn't.'

Slowly, his legs shaking, Max stood up. The cheering from down below rose in volume and then fell away into a hushed silence. Max shuffled closer to the end of the diving board.

The whole of **CRUSTY CRATER** was spread out below him. He saw all those unfinished Goozilla faces gazing up at him. Even from this height, he could make out the look of concern on the faces of his friends far below, and the smug expressions the **Sicklies** all wore.

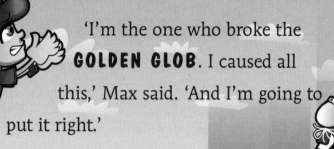

'I'm the one who broke the **GOLDEN GLOB**. I caused all this,' Max said. 'And I'm going to put it right.'

Raising his hands above his head, Max closed his eyes, bounced once, and jumped.

For a moment, he felt like he was soaring upwards, but then gravity took hold and he was falling. The air whooshed past him as he tumbled down, down, down towards the pool far below, still **TWISTING** and **ROLLING** as he fell.

SPLOOOSH!

Max belly-flopped into the pool. The slimy contents were launched up and outwards, and he heard the yelps and howls of the **Sicklies** as they were covered in goo.

Gasping, his head spinning from all the flips, Max heaved himself out of the pool. His friends rushed over and helped him to his feet, just as the REFBOT's screen displayed the scores one line at a time.

BUBBLE KITTEN

STYLE: 8
TECHNICAL ABILITY: 8
SPLOOSH: 4
TOTAL: 20

Bubble Kitten nodded and smirked as the Sicklies patted her on the back.

'That's good,' Gunk muttered.
'Annoyingly good.'

'Here's Max's score!' Gloop said, as the REFBOT's screen changed.

MAX

STYLE: 6
TECHNICAL ABILITY: 5

Bubble Kitten sniggered loudly. Max felt his shoulders sag. He'd let the Goozillas down. He'd failed them all.

SPLOOSH: 10

Max gasped. 'Wait, ten? That means . . .'

TOTAL: 21

'Wait, what?' Bubble Kitten yelped.

'Max, you did it!' cheered Gloop.

Max and the Goozillas **WHOOPED** and **BOUNCED** with excitement. They had won! The **WORLD OF SLIME** was saved.

But not for long . . .

CHAPTER NINE

TEAMWORK

'Hey, look!' said Gunk, pointing to Max's chest. Max looked down and saw a big golden medal hanging around his neck.

'You've got one, too,' Max said. Looking around, he saw medals appearing on all the Goozillas as the game crowned them the winners!

Atishoo landed in the **slime** behind them with a **BLURP**. When he jumped out, he wore a little medal of his own.

'Hey, cool!' he said, smiling proudly.

The ground beneath them rumbled again. The Goozillas and Max all looked down to see something rising up from beneath them. It was a winner's podium. The unfinished Goozillas clapped and whooped and cheered as best they could when Max and the others took their places.

As they stepped onto the podium the trophy cabinet containing the final **GLOB** piece swung open. Bubble Kitten made a sudden bound towards it.

'Enjoy your pointless little medals,' she sneered. 'Because I'll be taking the trophy!'

Reaching inside, she grabbed the last piece of the **GOLDEN GLOB** and held it to her chest.

'No!' Joe yelped.

'Say goodbye to your precious **GLOB** piece,' Bubble Kitten sneered. And then, with much huffing and puffing, she blew a protective bubble around herself and the other Sicklies. 'And say goodbye to the **WORLD OF SLIME**.'

'Stop her!' cried Max, as the wicked kitty rose into the air.

'How?' groaned Gunk. 'Even my gun won't blast a hole in that thing.'

They all watched, helplessly, as the bubble climbed higher and higher. It was out of reach now. Soon, the **GLOB** piece would be gone forever.

'Wait a minute,' said Max. 'I have an idea. Everyone gather round. We need all the Goozillas.'

'We're all here,' said Atishoo.

Max shook his head. 'No,' he said, looking out at the audience. 'I mean *all* the Goozillas!'

Bubble Kitten and the **Sicklies** drifted lazily on a breeze, the cramped bubble climbing higher and higher. They might not have won the **Gunge Games**, but it didn't matter. They had the final **GLOB** piece, and that was what counted. Now

97

they could take it somewhere, destroy it, and the volcano would be theirs for the taking. Bubble Kitten smirked. She could finally escape World of Pets forever.

No more horrible makeovers. No more cutesy-wootsy rainbows and cotton candy clouds. No more stupid costumes and flowery hats. She and the Sicklies would spend the rest of their lives living in the volcano, with an army of dried-out Goozillas as their slaves.

She was just planning where her bedroom was going to go when the hand caught her. It was a **BIG** hand. That was the first thing she noticed. **ENORMOUS**, even.

It was also slimy. **ENORMOUS**

and **slimy**, and wrapping its fingers around the bubble.

Just before the bubble was completely enveloped by the hand, the **Sicklies** looked down. All the Goozillas—even the weird ones with no faces from the audience— had **squidged** together to make a single

MASSIVE

figure. Near the top of its head was Max. His bottom half was buried in the **goo**, while his top half stuck out. He shouted instructions, and the giant figure seemed to be listening.

'Ooh this isn't good,' whispered Bubble Kitten, then the fingers tightened around the bubble, plunging the villains into darkness.

CHAPTER TEN

THE END?

'OK, now squeeze!' Max ordered.

A face emerged from the head of the giant Goozilla beside him. 'Yes, boss,' grinned Gloop, then he vanished again, sinking back into the mass of slimy bodies.

The **ENORMOUS** hand squeezed hard on the bubble. The villains had always insisted only Bubble Kitten's claws could pop one of the bubbles, but Max was betting it had never felt the pressure of several hundred Goozillas all squeezing at once.

A golden glow lit up the **slime** around

him. Max looked down to see the five other pieces of the **GOLDEN GLOB** all slotting themselves together below him, right in the centre of the giant's head. The **GLOB** was preparing, getting ready for—

Bubble Kitten's bubble **POPPED** in the giant's grip. The Sicklies coughed and spluttered as they were squished into its slimy palm. Max cheered as the final **GLOB**

piece was absorbed into the enormous
hand. The golden glow streaked down the
outstretched arm, past the shoulder, up the
neck, and then the whole world seemed to
be lit up by a blindingly bright light as the
giant Goozilla exploded back into hundreds
of smaller figures.

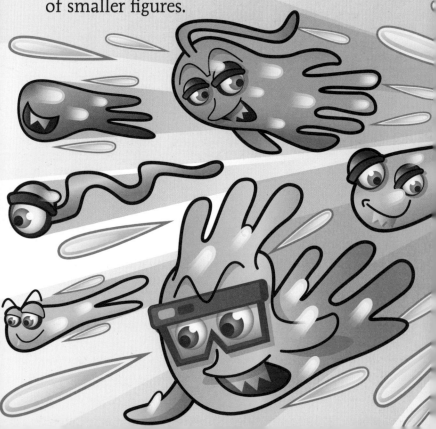

The next thing Max knew,
he was falling.

He tumbled down,
down,
down
towards the volcano,
and plunged straight through
the hole in the centre of the crater.

As he fell, he caught glimpses of
the levels he'd already visited. He saw
platforms, a tiny race track, forts, mazes,
and a beast-filled bog.

And then, Max landed on something soft. Lots of somethings soft, in fact. The Goozillas—his Goozillas—had linked arms and caught him before he hit the ground. The other nameless and unfinished creations lurked near the edges of the cavern.

'Better get out of the way,' Joe warned, pulling Max aside right before Bubble Kitten and the Sicklies landed on the floor with a series of thuds and at least one 'Ow.'

'Where is it?' demanded Bubble Kitten, jumping to her feet. 'Where is the . . . ?'

She stopped when she saw the fully intact GOLDEN GLOB floating in the air above its base. A hush fell over the volcano as the glowing orb lowered itself down

into position and locked
in place.

Everyone held their breath,
waiting to see what would
happen next.

Nothing changed.
The **slime** was still missing.
The volcano was still dry.

'Ha!' Bubble Kitten snorted.
'So much for your precious
Golden—'

A tower of **slime** erupted
from the floor beneath her,
launching her and the **Sicklies**
up, up, up through the volcano
again, and firing them out
through the hole at the top.

The Goozillas and Max all cheered and danced in the spray of glorious **gunge**, as the dark greys and browns of the volcano's walls became bright, vibrant greens.

'We did it!' Max gasped, barely able to believe it. A thick, gloopy blob of **ooze** splattered across his face and he laughed. 'We brought the **slime** back!'

The others joined in with the laughter. Max couldn't remember a time when he'd been happier. He had helped save his friends and their home, and now he knew how, there was nothing to stop him coming back to visit them any time he liked. He'd just have to be careful not to destroy the **GOLDEN GLOB** next time!

Which was just as well, because right then he heard the now familiar sound of his screen-time alarm. His time in the **WORLD OF SLIME** was over for another day, but this time he didn't mind. He knew there were plenty more adventures to come.

'See you tomorrow, guys?' he cried, as he felt the pull back to the real world.

'You'd better,' said Gloop.

'We'll be waiting,' added Joe.

Captain Crust and Gunk both saluted. Big Blob patted Max on the back, almost knocking him off his feet.

'See you, Max!' said Atishoo, then the world flipped over, and Max found himself back in his bedroom again.

And not a moment too soon. The door flew open and Amy ran in. 'It's my turn on the tablet!' she said. 'I heard the alarm.'

Max handed it over. 'Have fun with World of Pets,' he said, trying hard not to snigger at the thought of Bubble Kitten being poked and prodded and made to wear silly wigs.

Amy shook her head. 'What? Oh, no. I don't play that game anymore. It's boring.'

Max blinked in surprise. 'Don't you?' he said.

'No. I play a new one now. It's much better.'

'Oh,' said Max, not sure whether to be happy or disappointed. 'What's the new one?'

Amy grinned. 'World of Pets 2. It's got all new characters,' she announced, then she turned and skipped out of the room.

Max felt a twinge of worry as he watched her go. A new **World of Pets** game? Even with the **slime** back, new villains could be bad news for the Goozillas.

He shrugged. It was nothing they couldn't deal with. And besides, once he got the tablet back and set to work on those unfinished creations, the **WORLD OF SLIME** would have a few new characters of its own!

HAVE YOU READ THEM ALL?